BARBARA THROWS A WOBBLER

NADIA SHIREEN

JONATHAN CAPE • LONDON

Barbara was in a *very* bad mood.

BARBARA
THROWS A
WOBBLER

For Natasha

Some other books by Nadia Shireen

Billy and the Beast
Billy and the Dragon
The Bumblebear
The Cow Who Fell to Earth
Good Little Wolf
Hey Presto!
Yeti and the Bird

JONATHAN CAPE

UK | USA | Canada | Ireland | Australia | India | New Zealand | South Africa

Jonathan Cape is part of the Penguin Random House group of companies whose
addresses can be found at global.penguinrandomhouse.com.

www.penguin.co.uk
www.puffin.co.uk
www.ladybird.co.uk

 Penguin
Random House
UK

First published 2021

001

Printed in China

A CIP catalogue record for this book is available from the British Library

ISBN: 978–1–780–08136–6

All correspondence to:
Jonathan Cape, Penguin Random House Children's
One Embassy Gardens, 8 Viaduct Gardens, London SW11 7BW

MIX
Paper from
responsible sources
FSC® C018179
FSC
www.fsc.org

It had started
in the morning,
because of a
sock problem.

And at lunchtime
there had been a
strange pea.

Then Barbara stepped on a crack,
which she had been trying *very* hard not to do.
Things were going from bad to worse.

Her friends were frolicking in the park.

Hi, Barbara! said Martha.

Come and play! said Otto.

But Barbara didn't feel like a frolic.

Of course, Barbara had been in bad moods before.
She'd had huffs, grumps, upsets and strops.

But today was different.
Today felt like *a hundred* bad moods wrapped up in one.

And when **ANOTHER** terrible thing happened . . .

Barbara threw a GREAT BIG . . .

WOBBLER!

And then, suddenly, the Wobbler was actually THERE.
It loomed over Barbara's head.

"What's wrong with Barbara?" said Small Bob.
"And what's that weird thing?"

Nobody knew. The Wobbler hovered in the air.
Gloopy and heavy, like an angry jelly.

"Are . . . are you OK?" asked Otto.
But the Wobbler didn't want to talk.
So neither did Barbara.

"Would you like a cuddle?" asked Martha.
But the Wobbler was **not** accepting cuddles.
So neither was Barbara.

Barbara didn't even want any
of Small Bob's ice cream.
Which was really strange.

The Wobbler grew and grew and grew.
Soon it was the only thing that Barbara could see or feel.
She shook her fists and gave a great big yell.
But the Wobbler wasn't going anywhere.

"What if I'm stuck here forever?" thought Barbara.

"Let me GO!"
said Barbara.

"Let *ME* go!"
said the Wobbler.

"RAAAAARGH!"
she shouted.

"RAAAAARGH!"
shouted the Wobbler.

"Stinky bumhead!"
shouted Barbara.

"Stinky bumhead!"
shouted the Wobbler.

Barbara giggled.

"Stop copying me," said Barbara.
"I can't help it," it said. "I'm your wobbler. You made me!"

"I made you?" asked Barbara.
"Yes!" said the Wobbler cheerfully.

"You were really upset and angry and sad.
So here I am."

Barbara had a think. It *had* been quite a day.

Then she thought some more and said,
"Well, if I made you, can't I UN-make you?"

"Of course!" said the Wobbler.
"You're in charge."

So Barbara took a deep breath
and started to SQUISH the Wobbler down.

The Wobbler got smaller and smaller and smaller,
until Barbara could hold it in her paw.

"Goodbye, you strange little thing," she said.

"Oh, don't worry!" chirruped the Wobbler.
"I'll be back before you know it!"

Barbara saw that her friends were waiting for her.

"Are you OK?" asked Martha.

"I had a MASSIVE wobbler!" said Barbara. "But now I feel much less wobbly."

Barbara was *now* accepting cuddles.

(*And* ice cream.)

Barbara went back to the park to frolic with her friends.
Surely there wouldn't be any *more* wobblers today . . .

Would there?

BAD MOODS
(A Very Useful Guide)

fig.1: The Sulk
A quiet mood that often appears after losing a game or being refused treats.

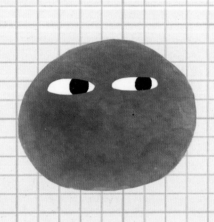

fig.2: The Tizzy
Usually noticed around bedtime or when a precious item has been lost.

fig.3: The Seethe
Angry but clever. Will quietly brew while thinking up rude names for people.

fig.4: The Huff
When something is *definitely* not your fault but everyone is saying that it's your fault.

fig.5: The Grump
Very, *very* sad and gloomy, not even a tickle under the armpit can cheer up a grump.

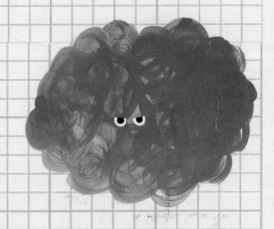

fig.6: The Wobbler
If you've already forgotten about wobblers, go back to the start of this book immediately.